Sweet Peas and Dahlias

(and other illustrated short stories)

Written by
Susan Alison

Illustrated by
Wendi Fyers

(Note from Monty: uh - four out of these five stories have dogs in them. Jus sayin. Zzzzzzzzzzzzz.)

Contents

For Helen xx

Sweet Peas and Dahlias

"What made…?"

"Why did…?"

They spoke at the same time, and laughed.

But Cathy was afraid to try again.

She felt jittery and breathless. She was excited – a feeling foreign to her these days.

Oh, if only Tom felt the same!

She looked away and saw Moocher gazing adoringly at her, his plumy tail waving slowly like a heavy flag. His eyes told her she was fine, that she should keep trying.

Taking a deep breath, she asked: "So, why _did_ you come here today?"

Tom flushed and switched his gaze to look past her.

She knew that over her shoulder he

would see the Malvern Hills. Over his

she could see the field they stood

in sloping up to a hedge of hawthorn,

ash, and oak trees stretching to the

sky.

It was exactly the same as all those years ago. Thirty years… Where had they gone?

Of course, they'd gone into Simon and the children. He'd meant so much to her in the end. He'd been right – his love had been enough for both of them when she felt she'd never love again.

Simon had been such a vigorous character and she felt it again when she visited his grave this morning.

She hadn't meant to call on him, but when she tried to walk to the park, Moocher pulled so hard on his lead that she found herself at Simon's side, wishing she had a bunch of sweet peas for him.

Sweet peas were his favourite

flower – he'd grown loads of them, all

different colours, some frilly, some not, all smelling of summer.

He'd been a passionate gardener. She was ashamed of the state she'd allowed his garden to get in. She did her best, but didn't have the heart for it.

Suddenly, a feeling of great unrest had filled her so sharply she jumped up and looked around. It was as though Simon was prodding her to go somewhere.

Moocher had barked as if to say, "Hurry up!"

"I don't understand what's happening, but I feel I should be somewhere else," she whispered, bending to pat Simon's grave. A warm feeling of approval filled her and she followed Moocher with a lightness of spirit she hadn't possessed since Simon died three years before.

When she got home her road map was on the kitchen table – open to the page that showed Malvern in Worcestershire.

She followed her instincts, feeling a fool, but telling herself no one need know what she was doing.

Now here she was.

"What made _you_ come here today?" Somehow, Tom had switched the question around again and she wondered how to answer.

She could say, "Well, my dead husband, in league with my dog, made me come here today", but she thought that might sound odd.

She could say she had come on a hunch, but that might sound even more odd given that she lived in Exeter – several hours down the motorway!

Wordlessly, she looked at him and wondered if he was going to say why _he_ was here.

But, of course, he could simply have been walking his dog like he had all those years ago when they first met.

She remembered it so well – their dogs had played together and wouldn't come back to their owners when called.

They met in the park again the following day.

On the third day he told her he was to be married in two months.

But she already knew she would never love anyone else the way she loved him. She was sure he felt it too, although no words were spoken.

They walked their dogs together for those two months.

She just kept turning up and he was always there.

She wanted to take what she could get while she could get it, even though she knew it would end in tears. They never even touched hands.

Then he married and she never saw him again.

Until today.

"Why did you marry her when you loved me?" The words were out before she realised she was going to speak them.

Tom didn't seem surprised by her question. He merely answered her as though he'd been wondering the same thing. "Back then, people _did_ marry if they promised they would," he said.

"Of course, Jeannette being ill clinched it. We didn't know at the time that she'd survive. She was diagnosed shortly after you and I met – otherwise I might not have…" He trailed off, a distant look in his eyes.

It was all so long ago.

"She's fine, though," he continued. "We brought up three lovely children. They're all leading their own lives now. Jeannette and I went our separate ways about three years ago. We're good friends, which is nice. She's getting married again. I live in Dundee now."

"Oh!" Cathy was surprised. "I thought you must still live here. Otherwise, how come you're here today?"

"That's the question I've been asking you. It's certainly odd. Unless..." He stopped.

"Unless what?" she prompted.

"What do you mean, you thought I lived here? If I had then surely we'd have bumped into each other. Don't _you_ live here either?"

She couldn't think what to say. The

coincidence was too enormous to swallow. Unless…

"Unless what?" she asked again.

"Did your dog bring you?" Tom asked. He seemed serious but had difficulty meeting her eyes. He looked at Moocher. "Your dog looks just the way I remember from before. But I suppose collies often do look similar."

"Yes, they do." Cathy looked at Tom's dog sitting next to Moocher and remembered his Rosie from back then – she'd been a pretty animal with an elegant tail, feathery legs and the sweetest expression. Her dog had fallen like a ton of bricks for Rosie, and Cathy had fallen for her master. Both Cathy and Moocher were heart-broken when Tom married.

"Did _your_ dog bring you?" Cathy asked.

Finally, Tom looked at her. He nodded.

They reached for each other at the same time. They embraced.

Over Tom's shoulder Cathy saw their two dogs greet Simon as he appeared. He patted them, and gave Cathy the thumbs-up sign.

"Do you like gardening, Tom?" Cathy asked, struck with a sudden thought.

"Yes. It's become my passion in recent years. I'll grow you dahlias that'll knock your socks off!"

Cathy saw Simon shrug in a 'can't-win-'em-all' kind of way.

He smiled at her and disappeared.

The end

Gotcha!

I saw them together. They'd be difficult to miss.

Both were well built, but Tim at six foot five, and Sheri at five foot three, made an odd couple.

Before they could spot me, I leapt onto the train two carriages down from where they were boarding.

I settled into my seat, having checked I wasn't in a 'quiet' carriage.

Sure enough, as soon as the train pulled out of the station everyone feverishly punched numbers into their mobiles and told people their journey had begun.

I waited until there was no way the train might slow down, go backwards and stop at the station again. I wanted to catch them red-handed.

I'd seen the way they looked at each other.

I wore dark glasses and a beret, of all things. I never wore hats, but this job called for one. And I was glad I was in disguise because my quarry had zig-zagged all over the station looking at this and that, buying odds and ends for the journey.

It's exhausting work following people and I was tempted to shore up my flagging spirits with a bar of chocolate, but I didn't.

We were well under way by now so I picked up my phone and rang Tim. I imagined how he'd feel when he saw it was me ringing. He'd feel guilty as hell. Good!

He didn't pick up straightaway. But then: his voice, subdued as if in a library, rather than loud and important like you usually get on a train: "Hello Mo, dear. How are you?"

"Fine thanks," I said. "How are things with you?" I was proud of how polite I was being considering the treachery I was witnessing.

"Fine, thanks..." he said. Then he paused. Then: "Mo, are you checking up on me?"

"Oh, Tim," I said, exaggerated patience in my voice. "Why would I want to do that?"

"I dunno. Just wondering. You ring a lot these days. Of course, I'm very happy to hear from you, but..."

He struggled for a bit until I let him

off the hook by changing the subject. "Have you forgotten it's our two monthiversary today, Tim?"

I couldn't believe he'd forget, but judging by the silence that greeted me, he must have done.

"No, I haven't forgotten," he said tightly.

"I thought we could celebrate it," I said. "Maybe have lunch together."

"Oh, dear. What a shame. I've got a really important meeting. Actually, you've disturbed me in it now. I have to go. I don't think I'll be out of here for a few more hours yet. We can catch up later. Must go. Byee."

I imagined him, two carriages up from me, wiping his face with a big red handkerchief and turning to Sheri pathetically.

"Phew," he'd say. "That was a close shave." She'd pat him on his arm and pop something delicious into his mouth and say something tepid like, "Oh, Tim. Don't worry. It's up to you what you do with your life."

Anger flooded me. How could he, with the wedding only nine weeks away?

I moved into the next carriage and paused to think things through.

I was sure he was cheating. Now he'd lied, too. Question was – how many times had he cheated? How many times had he lied?

I held my left hand up in front of me and wriggled my fingers. My engagement ring sparkled. I pulled it off with a curious satisfaction. Then I put it back again.

It was time to deal with this situation.

I moved up the train until I stood at the end of their carriage.

Then I rang him.

When he answered, he did so in a loud whisper: "Mo, for Pete's sake. I can't keep disturbing the whole meeting. I'm going to switch the phone off."

"Look up, Tim," I said.

"What?"

"Look up – towards the end of the carriage you're in."

"Carriage..? What do you mean..?"

"Look up."

His startled face slowly appeared around the edge of the seat in front of him. I waved at him – he disappeared.

I walked towards him. I knew he'd be cowering down in his seat, his frightened eyes appealing to Sheri for help. Would he brazen it out or simply confess?

When I drew level with their seat they looked at me, defiance clear on their faces. I glanced at their hands, but couldn't see them for a newspaper lying casually over their laps.

I leant forward and snatched the

paper away. Sure enough, they were holding hands. And their clasped hands rested on a veritable riot of chocolate bars and biscuits, half-eaten cakes and wicked, fattening things of all kinds.

"Gotcha," I crowed.

"I really did try, Mo," Tim said. "The

last two months have been absolute torture."

He looked so woebegone, I suddenly felt sorry for him. Truth is, that without his rivalry to goad me on I would never have succeeded so well with my own diet.

"Does it really matter if the best man's cuddly?" Sheri said. "I love him the way he is."

"So do I," I said, and gave my brother a kiss.

The end

The Proposition

Roger pulled his collar up as far as it would go and checked that no one looked in his direction. He walked along the pavement with a determined tread as though he had no doubts about where he was going this evening.

At least he knew it was a good area

for his purpose, having scouted it out the previous week.

He gazed downwards. This one was male, and decidedly belligerent by the looks of him. That was no good. Roger moved on.

This one was female and looked anxious to please, but she was too old.

Thank heaven this wasn't his patch. He could just imagine what would happen if he was recognized by any of his customers, or any of the lads from work. He'd never live it down. That was partly why he'd come here after dark. The damp, cold weather was a bonus. It kept other people off the streets.

This one was young enough, but she was dark, sullen and had an enormous, hairy mongrel lying across her lap. It lifted its head and bared yellow teeth. Roger hurried on.

In the office, if they knew he was doing this, there would be endless half-finished conversations which would include the phrase: "Why, Rog, you old dog, you!" Endless nudge, nudges and wink, winks along with manly slaps on the back.

This was the one.

She stared at him defiantly through a tangle of straw-coloured hair, knotted with neglect. She sat upright as though squaring up to him, and pulled her rags more closely around herself.

The salesman in him admired her presentation – her cleanly cut square of cardboard said, 'I'm Mandy and I'm homeless. Please help.' Somehow this made it more personal. He bet she got more money than the others. But he didn't want to just give her money.

"Come with me to the café," he said, nodding towards steamed-up windows across the road. "Let me buy you a meal."

She looked up at him, her lip curled in contempt. He knew he looked what he was: a lonely, middle-aged man with a slightly pronounced gut and a none-too-clean raincoat. "Please," he added, trying not to flinch at the gleam of stone set in her nose – an earring in the wrong place.

"Why should I? Why can't you give me the money instead?" she asked, her voice softer than he'd expected.

"I want to make sure you get a good meal," he said. "If I just give you the money you might not spend it on food and it's a cold night."

Why did she have to argue? Why couldn't she just say, 'yes' or 'no'?

"You think I'd spend it on drugs, don't you?"

He stared at her. The thought hadn't crossed his mind and he didn't know how to answer. He felt the tremor of nerves and was sorry he'd started this now. He'd rather pick up some fish and chips and go home to his empty house, home to his telly.

He backed off from her, his hands

up as if in surrender, mute with frustration and disappointment.

"Hold on," Mandy said. She jumped to her feet. Her blanket, some small coins, a pouch of rolling tobacco and papers, fell to the pavement. "Hold on. I didn't say no, did I? I'm coming. I'm coming."

Hastily she picked up her things and set off across the road. Roger went after her, hope blossoming in his chest. Maybe it _would_ be his lucky night after all.

She seemed oblivious to the

sudden hush in the café as they entered. She strode to a table and settled herself expectantly, snatching up the menu before Roger was seated and indicating almost immediately what she wanted.

Roger was conscious of the disapproving stares coming his way, but they were unimportant to him, easily ignored. This was his gamble, his risk and his life. They could mind their own business.

Emboldened, his voice was crisp as he ordered tea, steak pie, chips and beans twice from the girl who appeared by their table, a grubby notepad on a string at her waist, shocking pink bubble gum flipping around her mouth as she chewed and wrote out their order.

"So," Mandy said. "What's with you, then?"

"I beg your pardon," he said, his surge of confidence fleeing before the open curiosity in her gaze.

"Oh, you know…" She picked at her cuticles as though it was of life and death importance that she make her fingers even scabbier than they already were. "You with anyone?"

"I... I _was_ married." He could feel heat build up his neck and redden his face. His heart thumped a little bit harder. She must have guessed what he wanted. "But not any more."

"Oh? She die?"

"No. We split up. Family reasons. I'm divorcing her." He sighed and twisted his watch around his wrist and back again, wincing as the stretch metal links pinched his skin.

"And you," he asked, "What

happened to you?"

"That old story. You know the one. Wicked step-mother. Didn't get on. Left home."

"What about your father – didn't he try to stop you?"

The question hung in the air as the waitress placed heaped plates and steaming mugs in front of them, clattering cutlery onto the Formica surface, dropping little paper packets of salt in to a puddle of cold tea.

"I don't suppose he knew until too late. He was too busy doing his I'm-a-good-provider bit. He was completely wrapped up in his work."

Although she picked up her cutlery and held it in readiness, she continued: "Family stuff was women's business. Or I might be being too kind to him – maybe he just couldn't be bothered."

Roger winced at the bitterness in her voice, but felt the need to argue even though it might jeopardise his proposition.

"Hang on a minute," he said. "Hang on. He was probably trying to do his best for his family. He probably thought that if he spent his entire life working to keep them comfortable then they could sort out everything else. Did you ever try to say anything to him? It takes two, you know."

A flush gathered strength under her pale skin. "He was my father, my

Dad. He should have known." Her eyes dropped from his and she concentrated hard on emptying her plate.

"Pudding?" he said, a few minutes later, and was rewarded with a brief flash of white, even teeth.

He watched her put away chocolate sponge and custard. He wanted to ask her now before he completely lost his nerve. The need in him was so great he was amazed he could just sit there as he tried to work out how to phrase his wanting.

The scraping of the spoon on her bowl was like sandpaper on his nerves, leaving them raw and vulnerable.

It was terrifying to think that she might look him up and down contemptuously. Worse, she might scream her outrage at his suggestion. She might throw back her chair and point at him and tell the world what she thought of him.

He pushed his finger between his neck and his collar and tried to relieve the feeling of being throttled. He attempted a cough to clear his throat, but even that got stuck somewhere in his chest and sat there, radiating pain.

She'd finished her pudding and drained her mug. If he didn't say it right away, she would be gone. He _had_ to chance it now.

He leaned forward and trapped her hand between his own and the table.

"Mandy", he said, as freezing doubt poured into his heart and scalding sweat blurred his vision. "Mandy, will you come home with me?"

"Yes, Dad," she said. "I'd like that."

The end

He can't help it!

"Yeah," Shirley said. "He's her fourth. Fourth! It's too many, don't you think?"

"Well, I dunno," June said. "Our Vera had three…"

"Three's not so bad. But four…"

"Well, yeah. Maybe four is a bit over the top."

"Think of the disturbed nights."

"Yeah. She likes her sleep, too, but she'll spoil him rotten. She'll be up and down all night. She's always the same."

"Oh, surely not…"

"She will. I'm telling you – the bags under her eyes are half way down to her knees already."

"She's too soft for her own good, I reckon."

"I agree. She'll make a rod for her own back carrying on like that."

"Hmm. I know what you mean. Nice

to have the company though. I only had one." June looked wistful for an instant. "On the other hand, there's company and there's company, if you know what I mean..."

"Yeah, I know what you mean. Do you remember when we went round there that time when she had her third and couldn't hear ourselves speak for the racket he made? Some company." Shirley laughed and said, "He was pretty smelly too..."

June hiccupped a laugh before catching herself. "No more than usual…" she said.

"Pretty ugly, as well."

"Oh, Shirley," June protested. "What a thing to say!"

"But it's true. He's so ugly I can hardly bring myself to look at him."

"That's so unkind," June said. "Unkind. But true." They fell about laughing again, checking over their shoulders in case anyone they knew could hear them.

The only person showing any interest was the waitress. She was very keen on whipping away crockery just as soon as she could.

Shirley and June had got into the habit of leaving some of their second cups of tea to cool so they could stay longer.

They'd been in the Cakes R Us café so long today their tea nearly had skin on it.

"Let's push the boat out today, June," Shirley said. "Let's have another pot."

They were having such a good laugh, it was worth two pots of tea.

"And another cake," June said. "Let's go mad. Let's celebrate for her."

"Right. A celebration for her."

After they'd been served, Shirley looked sideways at June and said,

"He's bald as well."

June regarded her blankly. "They're all bald," she said.

"Well, yeah. But he's even more bald than the others."

"What, not even any fluff?"

"Nothing."

"What's she call him then? Planet Head? Billiard ball?"

They laughed until tears ran down their cheeks and the waitress looked so disapproving her face resembled nothing more than a mouldy walnut.

This set them off again and they

clutched the table to stop themselves falling off their chairs.

"Oh, God. You're such a card," Shirley said. "Such a card. Planet Head, indeed." She shook her own head and wiped her face with a handkerchief that trembled with still-bubbling mirth.

"Anyway, Planet Head wouldn't do. Or billiard ball, come to that," June said. "Have you noticed the shape of his head? It's more like an ice cream cone..."

Shirley had been in the act of

taking a sip of tea. She sprayed it across the table. June tried to jump back to avoid it with the result that she fell over with her chair in a huge clatter that had heads turning.

She didn't immediately get up. She couldn't. She was incapable with laughter.

"She says she loves the shape of his head. She says it was the very first thing about him that she clapped eyes on..." June choked before struggling to her feet. She hiccupped and swayed and had to support herself on the table before retrieving her chair and sitting down again.

"Really? What about his stomach, then? What shape would you call that? It looks like nothing so much as an upturned cup-cake to me…"

"He can't have been born like that. It'll be all her fault, not feeding him right. After all, how long has she had him?"

"Ooh, must be a couple of months…"

"Ah, well then. Time enough for him to have developed that. She isn't feeding him right, I tell you. Anyway, surely, it's more like a…, a…, more like he's pregnant himself."

"Oh, what a disgusting idea, June. How could you?"

"Maybe there's an alien in there. A chuntering alien all ready to leap out and take over the world." She was getting really carried away now. "That's what it looks like. He's pregnant."

"It'll hit the tabloids and they'll make a fortune…"

"I must protest! This is disgraceful behaviour," a new voice sliced through their flights of fantasy.

Shirley and June, startled, looked around to see that Mrs Cakes R Us had come out from behind the counter. She stood by their table and glared at them. "I expect the youngsters to behave like this, but two middle-aged _ladies_… It's utterly disgraceful!"

"Oh dear. I am sorry. It's just so funny…"

Mrs Cakes folded her lips nearly as hard as she folded her arms. She tapped her foot. The waitress stood behind her, duplicating her employer's stance and expression.

"I don't consider it at all funny to be making such cheap cracks," Mrs Cakes said. "No matter what he might look like, he can't help it."

Shirley and June looked at Mrs Cakes as though _she_ were an alien herself, looked at each other and fell into paroxysms of laughter again.

They were in no fit state to protest as Mrs Cakes and her outraged waitress propelled them out of the café.

They supported each other as they staggered down the street until Shirley suddenly stiffened and poked June in the ribs.

"Here she comes," she croaked. "And she's got him with her. We must make an effort to be nice. Just don't look at him." She coughed frantically, straightened up and smoothed her hair behind her ears.

She plastered a welcoming smile on her face and pretended to suddenly see her sister who walked proudly towards them, her pedigree American hairless terrier strutting at the end of a gold leash.

The end

Yours Worriedly...

Harry shuffled into the lounge, piled all the cushions on the settee and threw himself full-length, face down onto them.

His feet aired themselves over the other end of the sofa. One hand trailed on the floor; the other was trapped between him and the sofa.

Despite feeling the beginnings of pins and needles in his arm, it was a good place to do some serious grumping.

Sun streamed through the French

windows making the pattern in the carpet look like stained glass. It also spotlit lazy swirls of dust in the air. He'd have to get Margaret to do the vacuuming. And the dusting. Good grief! Surely it wasn't expecting too much for her to keep on top of these things.

Standards were falling around this place. He'd always insisted on a clean, ironed shirt every day and yet this morning when he'd gone to the airing cupboard there wasn't one. So he'd had to put on yesterday's. Now his neck itched.

His eyelids drooped and gradually closed only to snap open when a weight landed on his back. "Oof! Bowser, get off!" He twisted sideways and the little dog had to jump to the floor, but continued to bounce and growl. She caught Harry's trouser leg and worried it.

"I suppose you want a walk. Well, you'll have to wait 'til your mistress gets home." Harry levered himself upright, carried Bowser through the kitchen, and put her outside the back door where she hung about whining.

"Might as well get a coffee while I'm here," he muttered, fishing about in the sink for his favourite mug. Using the tips of his thumb and forefinger he liberated it from the mound of dirty dishes. He used the last of the coffee, having it black after sniffing the milk.

Grumping back into the sitting room he threw the cushions on the floor and sat on the settee, his feet up on a stool. He folded his arms and stared at the wall for a while, sighing mightily. There wasn't even a paper to read. What kind of a life was it when there wasn't a paper to read with his morning coffee?

The magazines in the rack were all so, so *womanish!* Of course, when *he'd* been working, he'd never had time for magazines. *He'd* had a responsible job. Why had they decided to do away with him? He'd been good at his job. Okay, he wasn't the only one made redundant, but that was no consolation…

He snatched up one of Margaret's magazines to avoid the familiar, circular thoughts. Opening it at random he decided it was just as well men were men and didn't have 'women's troubles'. He shivered in sympathy.

An article on the delights of garden open days around the country made him think maybe he should mow the lawn. Bowser nearly disappeared these days when she tried to walk across it, and had to bounce up and down to see over the grass.

A recipe for something you could do with a tin of salmon, eggs and potatoes sounded rather nice. Margaret could make that when she came in.

Then he reached the agony aunt

page.

And found that Margaret had betrayed him!

He couldn't believe what he read. He'd never forgive her. _Never_. All their friends were sure to see it and know it was about him. He was so horror stricken he didn't notice his coffee overturn and seep through the carpet. Bowser whined at the French windows. It was a spark to paraffin. "Oh, shut up! Shuddup!" Harry yelled.

Bowser, startled, ran off and hid in the lawn.

Margaret had disguised some of the facts so it wasn't obviously about him. But he knew. Oh, yes. _He_ knew.

If he hadn't picked up her magazine today she'd have got away with it, too.

Rage forced him from the sofa. Leaping up he hurled the magazine down onto the coffee-soaked carpet and jumped up and down on it. How could she do this to him?

Perhaps she hadn't. Perhaps he'd made a mistake. He retrieved the magazine to have another read. The letter said:

"Dear Agony Aunt, I have a problem with my husband. I love him dearly as I have for the last twenty-three years, but he was made redundant eight months ago and since then he's done nothing constructive. In fact, he just lazes around all day, grumping. He hasn't really put his heart into finding another job. He just goes on and on about how unjust it was that he lost the last job and how wonderful it all was then – when, in truth, he didn't enjoy it much anyway. He doesn't lift a finger to help around the house despite the fact that I have a full-time job and three children to get off to school everyday. Not to mention the three Yorkies he insisted on getting, but then left me to look after. I do love him, but I'm afraid his negative behaviour is going to wear our marriage down to nothing. What should I do? Yours worriedly, Mrs M."

No, no mistake about it. It _was_ him she was talking about. Okay, they'd been married thirty-seven years, not twenty-three. Admittedly, it wasn't eight months, it was four (and five days), and they didn't have three children, only two, and obviously they didn't have three Yorkies. Who'd want three of those yappy things for Pete's sake?

Yorkies…

Bowser!

Last seen cowering away from his enraged shout.

Shame engulfed him. What a way
to treat such a loving animal. He
hurried out to the garden, but it took
some time to persuade Bowser it was
safe to come out of hiding. Harry

cuddled her and gave her too many treats. She seemed to forgive him very quickly which increased his shame so much he mowed the lawn. It wasn't fair to such a short-legged animal to have grass so long.

Then, to Bowser's utter delight, Harry repeatedly threw her ball-on-a-rope until his arm ached. He rested by sorting out the shed which seemed to have got into a right mess.

He rushed down to the shops for some coffee, milk and a few other things that seemed a good idea.

Sitting with a fresh cup of coffee, he realised he could see the old one blotching the carpet. He scrubbed the spot and hoped that was the right thing to do with such stains.

He still couldn't believe Margaret's letter, so he re-read it expecting a renewed uprush of anger. Instead he felt a jolt of fear so great his legs went weak.

It was the way she'd spoken of their marriage wearing down to nothing.

If she was so desperate that she

was prepared to write to a national magazine for all to see, then this was serious indeed.

Harry wasn't good at doing nothing when he had a problem. Yeah, sure, he'd done nothing but grump around the place for the last few months, but that was, well… That was different.

This was different again. *This* was a crisis. His wife thought their marriage was in trouble. And it was his fault.

He leapt up and ran down to the shops again. He came back with flowers, chocolates, champagne and the local newspaper for the jobs section.

When Margaret came home she was greeted by an excited Bowser, the smell of home-cooking, a pile of freshly ironed shirts, an immaculate kitchen, and a grumpy Harry waving a magazine at her. "What do you think you're doing washing our dirty linen in public?" he demanded.

Bowser ran under the sideboard.

"What do you mean?" Margaret asked. She hadn't even got her coat off.

"I'm not stupid. I know you wrote this."

Margaret advanced on her husband and snatched the magazine from him. She read where he pointed.

Enlightenment dawned. "Oh," she said.

"Yes! Oh!" Harry said. "You thought I'd never see it, I suppose."

"Well…"

"Don't try to deny it."

"I wasn't…"

"It's outrageous, Margaret!"

Margaret hid her hand behind her back and crossed her fingers. "I…"

"It's time I faced up to what a drag I've been. Why couldn't you talk to me? Why did you have to ask an agony aunt, for Pete's sake?"

"I'm sorry, Harry. You seemed so distant." She hid her other hand and crossed the fingers on that one, too. The magazine fell to the floor.

"Well, I'm not any more. I've come to my senses. You don't even need to read the answer – whatever it was." Harry pounced on the magazine and ripped it to shreds, flinging the pieces over his shoulder. Bowser rushed out from underneath the sideboard and growled at a few of the scraps before viciously killing a particularly large one.

"I'm sorry I've been such a negative, uh, grumpy, person," Harry said. "I'll be different. Thank you for being here for me. Now I'll be here for you, too."

He reached for her. She had to uncross her fingers to put her arms around him. She cuddled her face into his neck and sent up an ecstatically grateful thought: *'Thank you. Oh, thank you, Worried Mrs M, whoever you are.'*

The end

About this collection of stories

The short stories in this book have been previously published in commercial publications in the UK and abroad.

These five stories have been published in the publications: The Weekly News, Yours, That's Life (Australia), Allas (Sweden) and Chat.

They are very short stories and mostly twist in the tale…

To add to your reading pleasure, they have been illustrated by the delightfully imaginative Wendi Fyers, who is sadly missed.

* * * * *

Susan Alison lives in Bristol, UK, and writes and paints full-time. She paints dogs, especially Border collies, corgis, whippets and greyhounds.

Every now and then she paints something that is not a dog just to show she's not completely under the paw – mainly, she's under the paw...

Short stories of hers (*not* usually about dogs) have been published in women's magazines worldwide. Her romantic comedy: 'White Lies and Custard Creams' became a bestseller on Amazon.

See Amazon for all her romantic comedies, urban fantasy novels, colouring books (traditional line art, and greyscale), notebooks, illustrated doggerel etc; see her website at www.SusanAlison.com for more news of books and artwork, which can also be found in her Etsy shop at SusanAlisonArt.Etsy.com in which fine art prints, greeting cards, coasters etc are available.

White Lies and Custard Creams

#1 best-selling romantic comedy with a dash of mystery

All His Own Hair

#1 best-selling romantic comedy with a dash of sabotage

Greyscale colouring books!

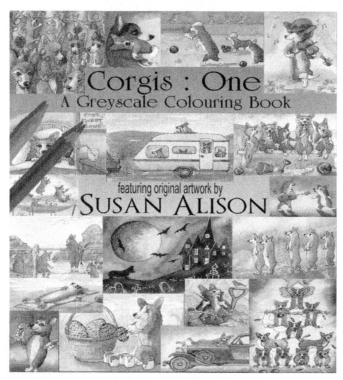

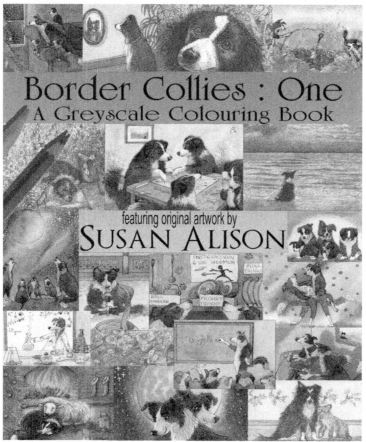

Also by Susan Alison and available now…

Colouring Books – traditional line art:
Corgis Rule!; Corgis Rule Again!
Carousing Cats!; Brilliant Border Collies!
Great Greyhounds & Wonderful Whippets; Christmas Canines

Colouring Books - greyscale:
Corgis : One; Corgis : Two
Border Collies : One; Greyhounds and Whippets : One
Cats and Kittens : One

Urban Fantasy Novels:
Hounds Abroad, Book One: The Lost World
Hounds Abroad, Book Two: World Walker
KATIE FFORDE: *"Magical! Full of warmth and humour."*

Romantic Comedies:
White Lies and Custard Creams; All His Own Hair
Out from Under the Polar Bear; New Year, New Hero
JILL MANSELL: *"Susan Alison has written a lovely, quirky romp packed with off-the-wall characters - original, intriguing and great fun!"*

Illustrated Doggerel:
The Corgi Games; Woofs of Wisdom on Writing

Short Stories:
Sweet Peas and Dahlias (and other illustrated short stories)

Notebooks:
Blank sheet music – Musicians' notebook – Basset Hound playing violin
Notebooks for doodling and for writing: Half-blank, and half-ruled pages – for doodlers and for writers! And corgis.
Other large print books and notebooks are on their way
* * * * *

See artwork and books at www.SusanAlison.com;
or @bordercollies on Twitter,
or search for Susan Alison (one 'L') on Facebook.

See artwork and books at www.SusanAlison.com
or @bordercollies on Twitter
or search for Susan Alison (one 'L')
on Facebook.

Printed in Great Britain
by Amazon

59610107R00057